Do Lions Hate Haircuts?

BETHANY WALKER   ILLUSTRATED BY STEPHANIE LABERIS

To Elsie and Lonnie –
thanks for not being little
Leonards for your haircuts!
With all my love – B.W.

To Rebecca, for making me
look fabulous every single
time I sit in that salon chair!
– S.L.

WALKER BOOKS
AND SUBSIDIARIES
LONDON · BOSTON · SYDNEY · AUCKLAND

First published 2022 by Walker Books Ltd, 87 Vauxhall Walk,
London SE11 5HJ • Text © 2022 Bethany Walker • Illustrations
© 2022 Stephanie Laberis • The right of Bethany Walker and
Stephanie Laberis to be identified as author and illustrator
of this work respectively has been asserted by them in
accordance with the Copyright, Designs and Patents Act 1988
This book has been typeset in Archer Medium • Printed in China
All rights reserved. No part of this book may be reproduced,
transmitted or stored in an information retrieval system in
any form or by any means, graphic, electronic or mechanical,
including photocopying, taping and recording, without
prior written permission from the publisher. British Library
Cataloguing in Publication Data: a catalogue record for this book
is available from the British Library • ISBN 978-1-4063-8841-1
www.walker.co.uk • 10 9 8 7 6 5 4 3 2 1

This is Leonard the Lion.

King of the beasts!
Master of the savannah!
Leader of his pride ...

and a great big baby when it's time for a haircut!

From the tips of the tallest trees to the bottom of
the deepest watering hole, Leonard had searched
his kingdom for a hairdresser he liked.

But Leonard hated haircuts and knew he always would.

"Too chompy!"

"Too stompy!"

"Too beaky!"

"Too cheeky!"

No one was quite right.

But one day, a mouse called Marvin bravely offered to help.
"You?" huffed Leonard. "You're far too small to be a hairdresser."
"Nonsense," said Marvin.
"Just look what I can do!"

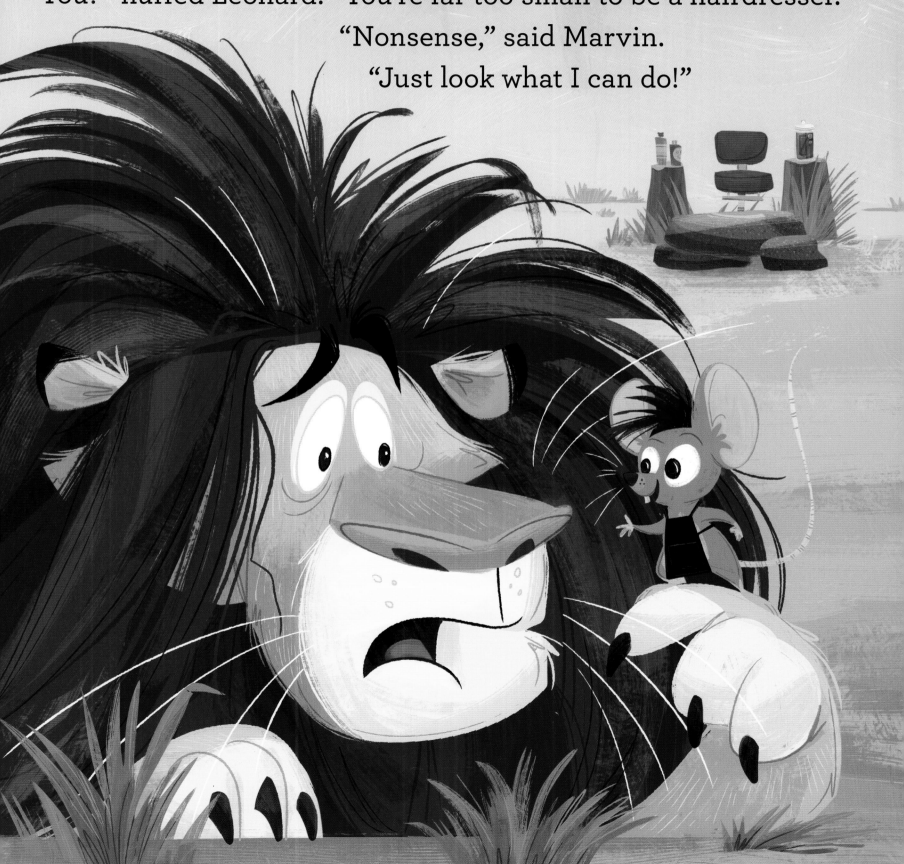

"Hmmm," purred Leonard.

"Ahhhh," sighed Leonard.

"Hee hee," giggled Leonard.

Marvin held his breath.
What would Leonard
think of his new haircut?

Hairstyle after hairstyle, Marvin worked his magic on Leonard's mane. With each new look, Leonard felt on top of the world!

Soon, Marvin wasn't just Leonard's hairdresser —
he was his best friend, too.

Leonard was happy and all was peaceful in the kingdom.
Then one day, as he was returning to the pride,
Leonard smelled something FAMILIAR in the air.

"Hmmm,"
he heard.

"Ahhhh,"
he heard.

"Hee hee,"
he heard.

"Noooooo!" wailed Leonard.
"You can't cut *her* hair. You're *MY* hairdresser.
You're *MY*... friend!"

Fighting back tears, Leonard decided never
to get his hair cut EVER AGAIN.
So as the weeks went by,
Leonard's hair grew and grew.

And the longer his hair grew, the sadder Leonard became.

And the sadder he became, the more Leonard missed his friend.

Leonard's family tried to help.
"Why don't you just find Marvin and say sorry
for being jealous?" suggested Leonard's cub.

But Leonard refused to listen.

Then, from out of nowhere, he heard a ...

SQUEEEEEEEAAAAAAAAAAAAARAAAAAAAKKK!

I know that squeak, thought Leonard.
Marvin is in danger!

"I'm coming, Marvin!"
roared Leonard.
But as he ran,
he tripped ...

and he fell ... "Argh!"

And he rolled ...

"Eeek!"

And he ...

landed. Ooof!

He was a bit bumped and bruised, but Leonard
had saved his friend. "I'm sorry, Marvin," he said.
"I have been the *nitwit* of the beasts, the *noodle* of
the savannah, the *nincompoop* of —"

"That's OK, Leonard," interrupted Marvin with a giggle.
"but when an animal wants a top-notch haircut,
I cannot let them down."
Leonard smiled. "You have just given me an IDEA!"

Just a few weeks later, it was the grand opening ...

Leonard had set up the very first
hairdressing school on the savannah!
"Now you can teach other hairdressers, Marvin, and
everyone can have fabulous haircuts!" Leonard beamed.

"Too beaky?"

"Too cheeky?"

With Marvin to guide them, hairdressers across the land learned showstopping skills.

The school was a roaring success.
Even Marvin got the haircut
he'd always dreamed of!

And Leonard really did feel like the leader
of his pride, master of the savannah, and ...

KING OF THE DANCE FLOOR!

Everyone in Leonard's kingdom was happy ...

UNTIL ...

"Leonard, it's time to have your nails clipped!"